W9-BJK-984

The Snow Angels' Christmas

MJ Michaels

Illustrated by **Kathy Nausley**

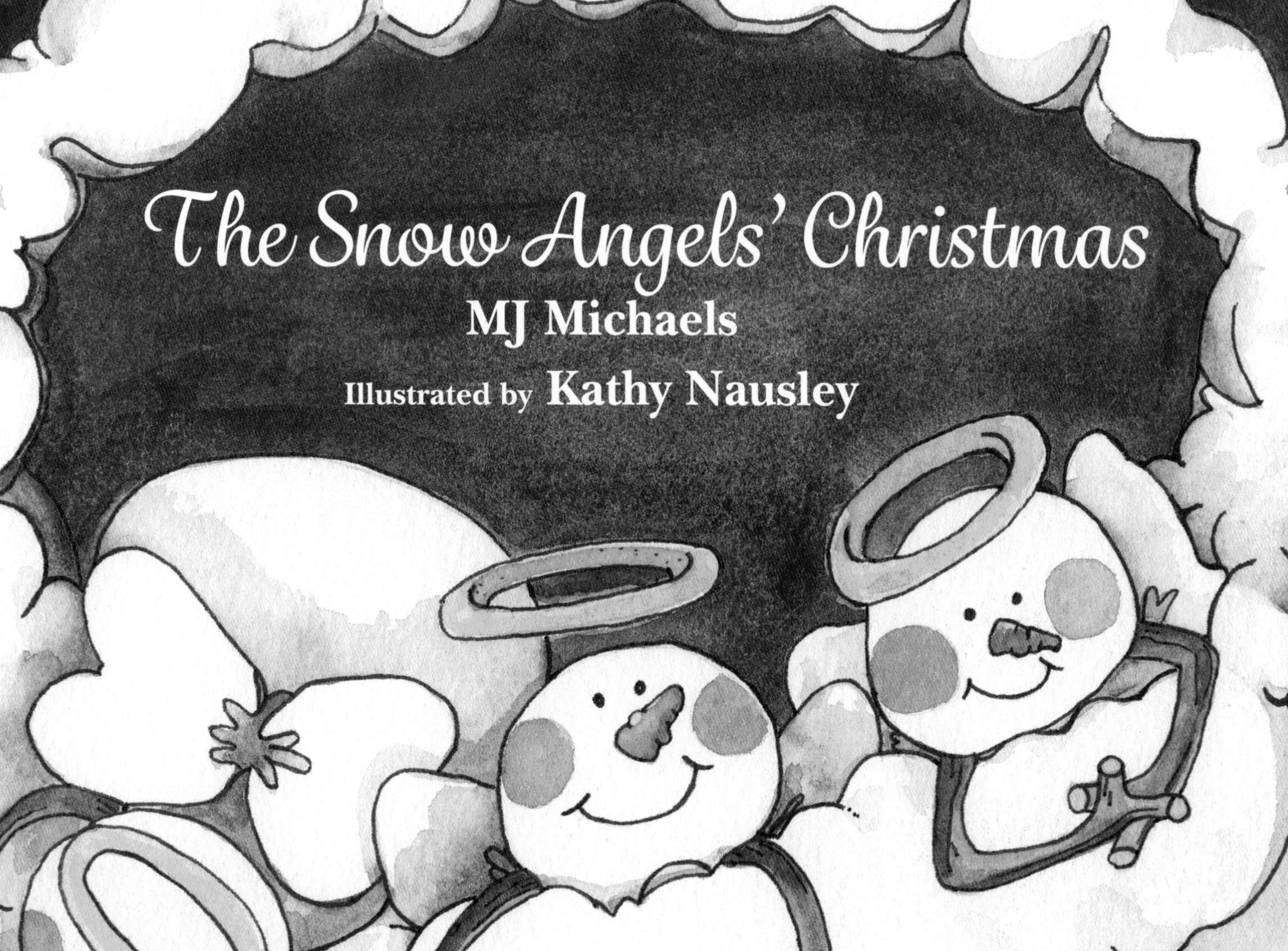

SEA GRASS

To my angels – Paul, Addison, Nicholas and Michael. – MJM
To Ellie, who makes my heart smile. – KN

Quarto is the authority on a wide range of topics.
Quarto educates, entertains, and enriches the lives of our readers—enthusiasts and lovers of hands-on living.
www.quartoknows.com

Published by Seagrass Press,
a division of Quarto Publishing Group USA Inc.

Design: Nicholas Tiemersma
Cover Image: Kathy Nausley
Illustration: Kathy Nausley

SEA GRASS
6 Orchard Road, Suite 100
Lake Forest, CA 92630
quartoknows.com
Visit our blogs at quartoknows.com

Printed in China
1 3 5 7 9 10 8 6 4 2

FSC www.fsc.org MIX Paper from responsible sources FSC® C017606

As the Snow Angels watched over the town of Nazareth, all looked calm, all looked bright.

The Snow Angels had heard that the Roman Emperor wanted to have a list of all the people. Mary and Joseph would have to travel to Bethlehem.

The Angels were worried. Mary was with child and the trip would be long and difficult. The Angels put their halos together to come up with a plan to help.

Quickly they went to Nazareth to see how Mary and Joseph were doing. Joseph was comforting Mary. He knew the trip to Bethlehem would be difficult, but he was certain that everything would be all right.

Mary prepared by gathering everything needed for the journey. The Angels rolled up their sleeves and got to work!

The next day, Mary and Joseph were on their way. The little donkey worked hard but not as hard as the Snow Angels!

Finally, the little town of Bethlehem! There were so many people. Every house was full, every bed was taken. The only shelter they could find was in a stable.

The Snow Angels got busy. They lit the lamps and swept away all of the cobwebs. The Angels fluffed the hay to make a soft resting place; they even told the animals they must behave. After all, this is where the baby would be born.

Joy to the World!

One by one the Snow Angels entered the stable. Wrapped in swaddling clothes, lying in the manger – they saw Baby Jesus. Oh, what a heavenly sight!

The Snow Angels flew north, south, east and west excited to spread the news. They shouted from the mountain tops so that all could hear,

"We bring tidings of great joy.
Behold, the child is born!"

The world – and the Snow Angels – rejoiced!